# The Age of Dinosaurs

# Meet Iguanodon

Written by Mark Cunningham

Illustrations by Leonello Calvetti and Luca Massini

Cavendish Square

New York

Published in 2015 by Cavendish Square Publishing, LLC
243 5th Avenue, Suite 136, New York, NY 10016

Copyright © 2015 by Cavendish Square Publishing, LLC

First Edition

Website: cavendishsq.com

CPSIA Compliance Information: Batch #WS14CSQ

All websites were available and accurate when this book was sent to press.

Library of Congress Cataloging-in-Publication Data

Cunningham, Mark, 1969- author.
Meet Iguanodon / Mark Cunningham.
pages cm. — (The age of dinosaurs)
Includes index.
ISBN 978-1-62712-788-2 (hardcover) ISBN 978-1-62712-789-9 (paperback) ISBN 978-1-62712-790-5 (ebook)
1. Iguanodon—Juvenile literature. I. Title.

QE862.O65C864 2015
567.914—dc23

2014001526

Editorial Director: Dean Miller
Copy Editor: Cynthia Roby
Art Director: Jeffrey Talbot
Designer: Douglas Brooks
Photo Researcher: J8 Media
Production Manager: Jennifer Ryder-Talbot
Production Editor: David McNamara
Illustrations by Leonello Calvetti and Luca Massini

The photographs in this book are used by permission and through the courtesy of:
JuliusKielaitis/Shutterstock.com, 8; catolla/Shutterstock.com, 8; skyfish/Shutterstock.com, 8; wassiliy-architect/Shutterstock.com, 8; Unknown/File:Gideon Mantell.jpg/Wikimedia Commons, 20; Drow male/File:Iguanodon bernissartensis (replica).001 - Natural History Museum of London.jpg/Wikimedia Commons, 21.

Printed in the United States of America

# CONTENTS

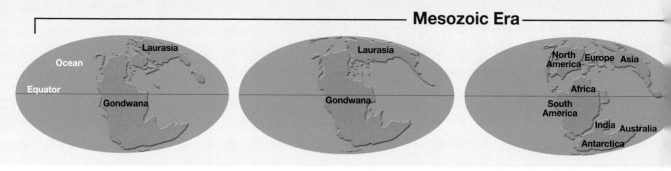

**Mesozoic Era**

Late Triassic
227 – 206 million years ago.

Early Jurassic
206 –176 million years ago.

Middle Jurassic
176 – 159 million years ago.

# A CHANGING WORLD

Our planet Earth is more than 4.6 billion years old, and one of the most interesting times in Earth's history is the time of the dinosaurs.

The word "dinosaur" comes from two Greek words—*deinos* and *sauros*—that translate to "fearfully great lizards."

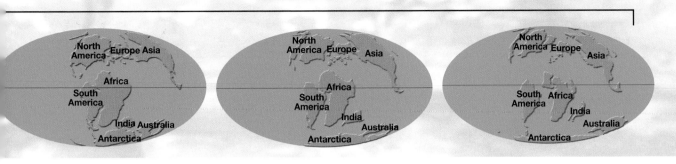

| Late Jurassic | Early Cretaceous | Late Cretaceous |
|---|---|---|
| 159 – 144 million years ago. | 144 – 99 million years ago. | 99 – 65 million years ago. |

Earth is so old that its history is divided into geological time, with eras, periods, epochs, and ages. The dinosaur era, called the Mesozoic Era, is divided into three periods: Triassic, which lasted 42 million years; Jurassic, 61 million years; and Cretaceous, 79 million years. Dinosaurs ruled the world for over 160 million years.

People and dinosaurs were never on the planet together. Dinosaurs disappeared nearly 65 million years before we first appeared on Earth.

The dinosaur world was very different from the world today. The climate was warmer, the continents were different, and grass did not even exist!

5

# A GENTLE VEGETARIAN

A member of the *iguanodontidae* family, Iguanodon (pronounced ih-GWAN-oh-don), meaning "iguana tooth," was in the order of *ornithischia*, meaning "bird-hipped" dinosaurs, and the suborder of *ornithopoda*, meaning "bird feet." These orders were among the most highly evolved group of dinosaurs that lived between the beginning of the Jurassic and the Late Cretaceous periods, from 190 to 65.5 million years ago. Paleontologists have studied Iguanodon more than any other dinosaur.

Iguanodon, a herbivorous (plant-eating) dinosaur, roamed every continent except Antarctica about 150 million years ago during the early to mid-Cretaceous period. Although the dinosaur was a quadruped, meaning that it walked on four legs, it would also move on two legs (bipedal) from time to time. Paleontologists believe that when chased by predators, Iguanodon was capable of running on its hind legs, but only for a short distance. Its maximum speed was about 15 miles (24 kilometers) per hour.

Iguanodon bore foot-long spikes at the end of its thumbs. The front of its beak-shaped mouth was toothless. The dinosaur measured up to about 30 feet (9 meters) in length and up to 16 feet (5 m) in height. It weighed as much as 10,000 pounds (4,500 kilograms). Despite this, paleontologists describe it as a "gentle plant eater."

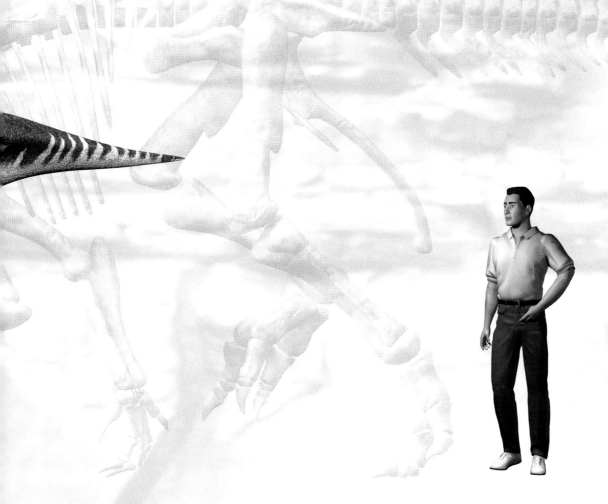

# FINDING IGUANODON

Iguanodon roamed throughout the continents of Europe (England, France, Germany, Belgium, and Spain) and North America (Utah and South Dakota) about 150 million years ago during the early to mid-Cretaceous period. Because of the dinosaur's early discovery, paleontologists referred to it as a "wastebasket genus," meaning that any dinosaur that remotely resembled Iguanodon was assigned as a separate species. However, there is only one proven species of Iguanodon, the *I. bernissartensis*.

England

Germany

Belgium

Utah

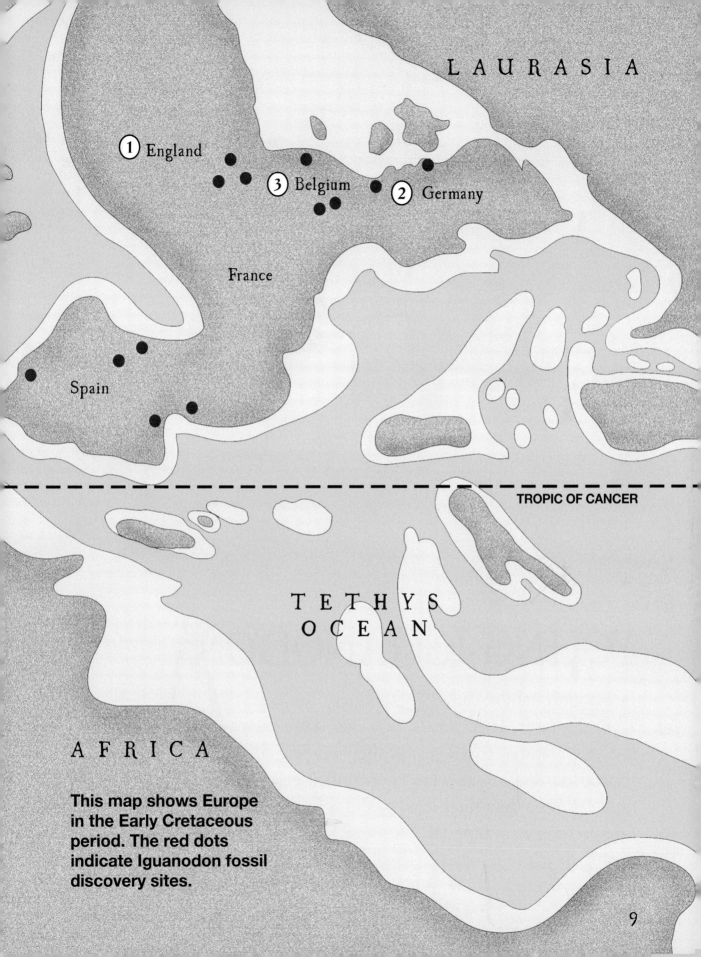

L A U R A S I A

① England

③ Belgium

② Germany

France

Spain

TROPIC OF CANCER

T E T H Y S
O C E A N

A F R I C A

This map shows Europe
in the Early Cretaceous
period. The red dots
indicate Iguanodon fossil
discovery sites.

# YOUNG IGUANODON

Iguanodon babies, called "hatchlings," were smaller versions of the adult dinosaur. Their heads, however, were proportionately larger in size compared to the rest of their bodies. Also, their snouts were shorter, and their eyes were enormous. Because their arms were much shorter than their legs, paleontologists believe that baby Iguanodons were bipedal. This may have helped them to quickly escape their predators. No fossils of Iguanodon nests or babies have been uncovered.

# DANGEROUS PLACES

Iguanodon lived along the edges of swamps and marshes, and in woodland areas. Within these environments were dangers that included quicksand and crocodiles. Iguanodon was large and heavy. The dinosaur's hands touched the earth with its fingers only, not with its entire palm. All this often made it difficult for Iguanodon to move quickly when predators, such as Tyrannosaurus Rex and Megalosaurus, roamed about. Iguanodon's best weapon was its sharp thumb spike, which could deeply pierce the flesh of any enemy.

# MEALTIME

Iguanodons likely lived in herds that moved about continuously and foraged for food. They used their toothless beak to pull plants, which they chewed with the teeth of their upper and lower jaw. An ample cheek pouch kept the food from sliding out of their mouths.

While the smaller Iguanodons only ate plants and leaves from the bottom of trees, the adults could rise on their hind legs and reach the higher branches.

# UNDER ATTACK

Southern England 125 million years ago was a very dangerous place for such a gentle vegetarian as Iguanodon. Various species of carnivorous dinosaurs were lying in wait, and could attack and kill the plant eaters at any time. The aging or sick members of the dinosaur herd, as well as the young and helpless, were especially vulnerable.

# INSIDE IGUANODON

From the side view, Iguanodon's skull appears low and long, resembling that of a horse. The dinosaur's teeth were leaf-shaped with ridges, but the chewing of tough plants often wore down the surface of its teeth. Iguanodon had up to twenty-nine rows of teeth in its upper jaw and up to twenty-five in the lower jaw. Its hind legs were large and powerful. Its hind feet had three toes, but did not have the sharp claws of the meat-eating dinosaurs.

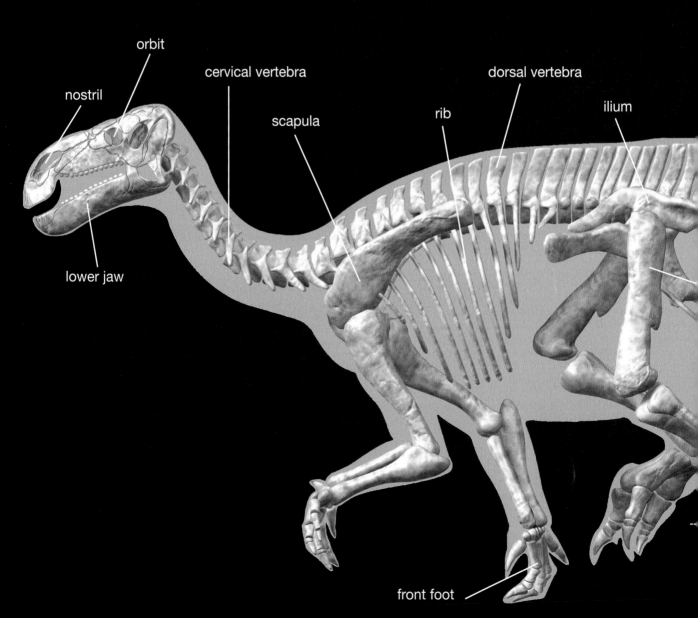

orbit

cervical vertebra

dorsal vertebra

nostril

ilium

scapula

rib

lower jaw

front foot

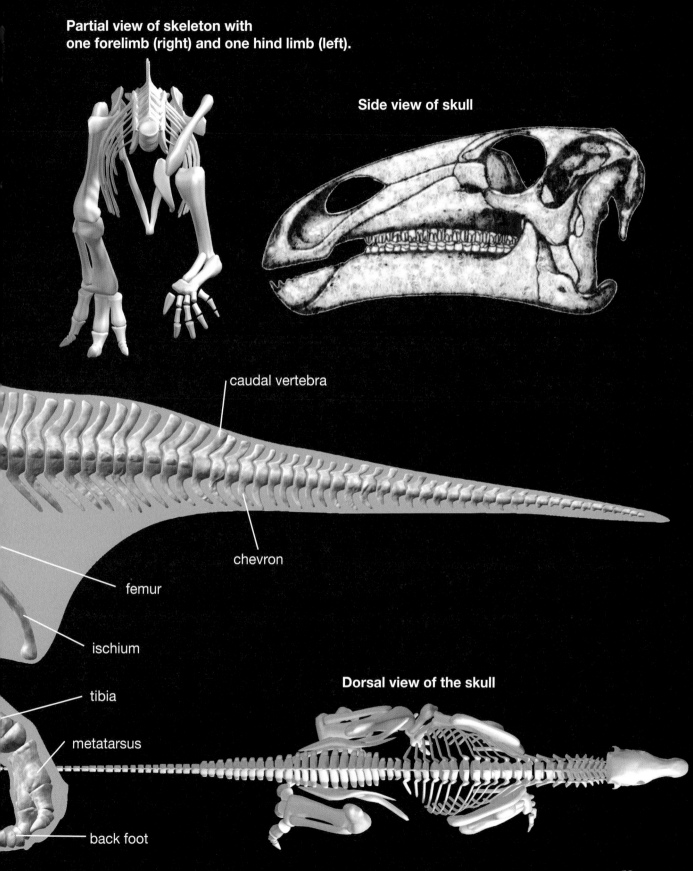

**Partial view of skeleton with one forelimb (right) and one hind limb (left).**

**Side view of skull**

caudal vertebra

chevron

femur

ischium

tibia

metatarsus

**Dorsal view of the skull**

back foot

# UNEARTHING IGUANODON

Iguanodon fossils were among the first herbivorous dinosaurs to be unearthed. British paleontologist Gideon Mantell and his wife, Mary, discovered a tooth and a few bone fragments belonging to the dinosaur in 1822 along a roadside in Sussex, United Kingdom. At that time, dinosaurs had still not been recognized. These fossils resembled the structure of a modern-day iguana. Mantell named the dinosaur "iguana-tooth" because with his initial findings, he thought of Iguanodon as an ancient lizard, not a dinosaur. In fact, he initially wanted to name Iguanodon "Iguanasaurus."

**Gideon Mantell and his wife, Mary, were the first to discover Iguanodon remains.**

A six-inch spiked bone was also unearthed. Paleontologists assumed that this spike protruded from Iguanodon's nose. However, in later discoveries it was identified as a thumb claw that the dinosaur likely used in self-defense.

Iguanodon skeletons have also been unearthed in Belgium and Germany. These nearly complete fossils were jumbled into piles. This suggests that Iguanodon traveled in small herds that may have been trapped in a flash flood, or drowned while attempting to cross a flooded river.

Other Iguanodon fossils have been unearthed throughout Europe, and in Utah and South Dakota. The largest collection, more than thirty-five, was discovered in a Belgian coalmine in 1878. These findings greatly helped scientists better understand Iguanodon.

A complete Iguanodon skeleton.

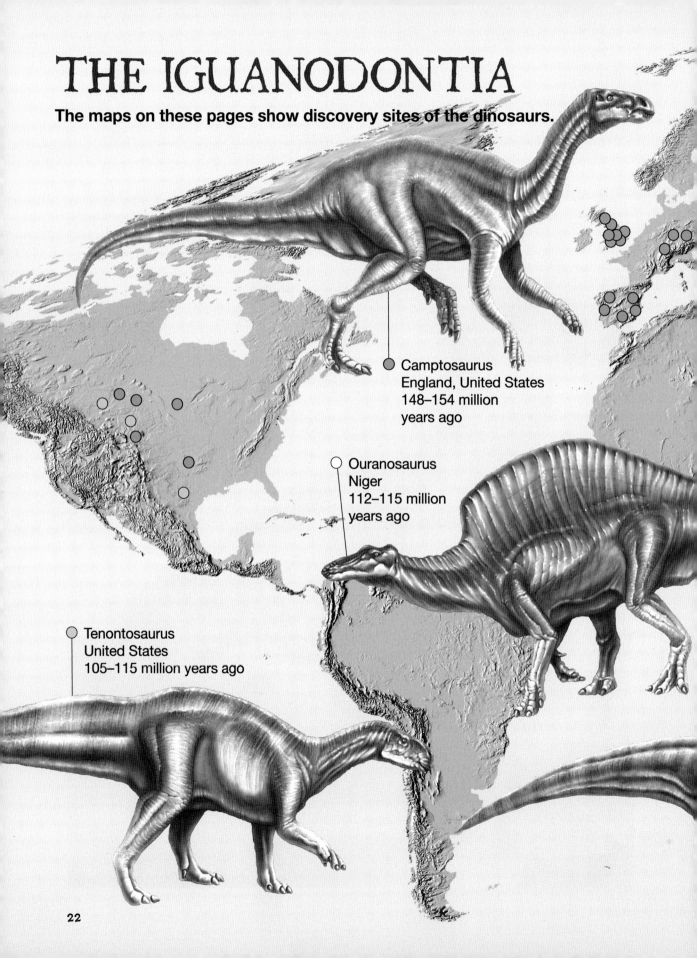

# THE IGUANODONTIA

**The maps on these pages show discovery sites of the dinosaurs.**

Camptosaurus
England, United States
148–154 million
years ago

Ouranosaurus
Niger
112–115 million
years ago

Tenontosaurus
United States
105–115 million years ago

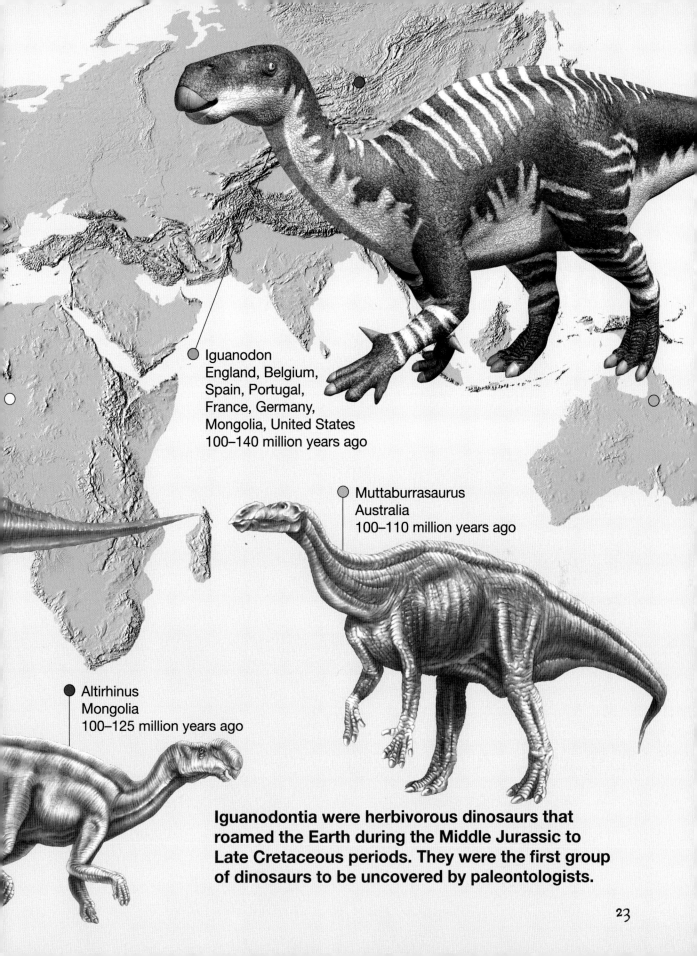

Iguanodon
England, Belgium,
Spain, Portugal,
France, Germany,
Mongolia, United States
100–140 million years ago

Muttaburrasaurus
Australia
100–110 million years ago

Altirhinus
Mongolia
100–125 million years ago

**Iguanodontia were herbivorous dinosaurs that roamed the Earth during the Middle Jurassic to Late Cretaceous periods. They were the first group of dinosaurs to be uncovered by paleontologists.**

23

# THE GREAT EXTINCTION

The dinosaurs disappeared from Earth about 65 million years ago. Scientists hypothesize that a large meteorite hitting the earth caused this extinction. A wide crater caused by a meteorite exactly 65 million years ago has been located along the coast of Mexico. The dust suspended in the air by the impact would have limited sunlight, causing temperature to drop significantly, killing many plants.

Without their food supply, plant-eating dinosaurs would have starved or frozen to death. Smaller numbers of plant-eating dinosaurs would have starved meat-eating dinosaurs. However, some scientists believe dinosaurs did not die out completely and that present-day chickens and other birds are, in a way, the descendants of the large dinosaurs.

# A DINOSAUR'S FAMILY TREE

The oldest dinosaur fossils are 220–225 million years old and have been found all over the world.

Dinosaurs are divided into two groups. Saurischians are similar to reptiles, with the pubic bone directed forward, while the Ornithischians are like birds, with the pubic bone directed backward.

Saurischians are subdivided in two main groups: Sauropodomorphs, to which quadrupeds and vegetarians belong; and Theropods, which include bipeds and predators.

Ornithischians are subdivided into three large groups: Thyreophorans, which include the quadrupeds Stegosaurians and Ankylosaurians; Ornithopods; and Marginocephalians, which are subdivided into the bipedal Pachycephalosaurians and the mainly quadrupedal Ceratopsians.

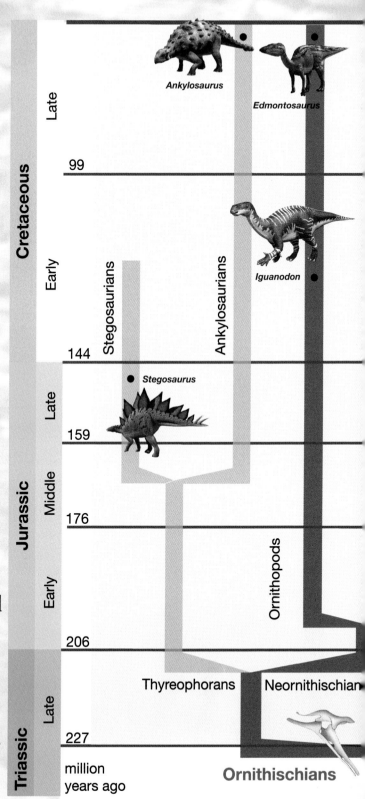

Ankylosaurus

Edmontosaurus

Iguanodon

Stegosaurus

Stegosaurians

Ankylosaurians

Ornithopods

Thyreophorans

Neornithischian

Ornithischians

Cretaceous

Late

99

Early

144

Jurassic

Late

159

Middle

176

Early

206

Triassic

Late

227

million years ago

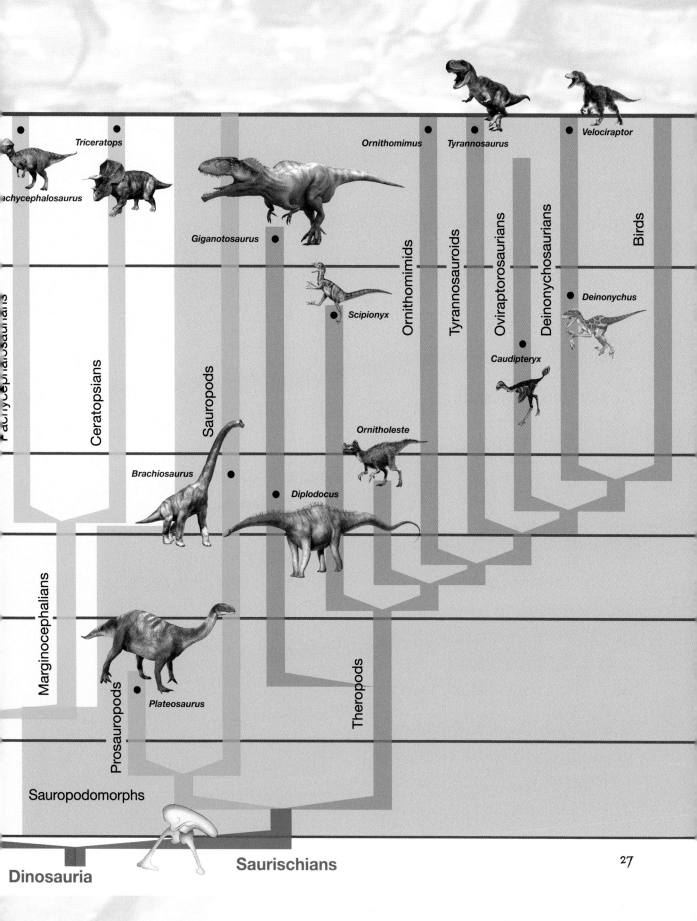

Triceratops

Pachycephalosaurus

Ornithomimus

Tyrannosaurus

Velociraptor

Giganotosaurus

Ornithomimids

Tyrannosauroids

Oviraptorosaurians

Deinonychosaurians

Birds

Pachycephalosaurians

Scipionyx

Deinonychus

Ceratopsians

Sauropods

Caudipteryx

Ornitholeste

Brachiosaurus

Diplodocus

Marginocephalians

Theropods

Prosauropods

Plateosaurus

Sauropodomorphs

**Dinosauria**

**Saurischians**

27

# A SHORT VOCABULARY OF DINOSAURS

**Bipedal**: pertaining to an animal moving on two feet alone, almost always those of the hind legs.

**Bone**: hard tissue made mainly of calcium phosphate; single element of the skeleton.

**Carnivore**: a meat-eating animal.

**Caudal**: pertaining to the tail.

**Cenozoic Era (Caenozoic, Tertiary Era)**: the interval of geological time between 65 million years ago and present day.

**Cervical**: pertaining to the neck.

**Claws**: the fingers and toes of predator animals end with pointed and sharp nails, called claws. Those of plant-eaters end with blunt nails, called hooves.

**Cretaceous Period**: the interval of geological time between 144 and 65 million years ago.

**Egg**: a large cell enclosed in a porous shell produced by reptiles and birds to reproduce themselves.

**Epoch**: a memorable date or event.

**Evolution**: changes in the character states of organisms, species, and higher ranks through time.

**Extinct**: when something, such as a species of animal, is no longer existing.

**Feathers**: outgrowth of the skin of birds and some dinosaurs, used in flight and in providing insulation and protection for the body. They evolved from reptilian scales.

**Forage**: to wander in search of food.

**Fossil**: evidence of life in the past. Not only bones, but footprints and trails made by animals, as well as dung, eggs or plant resin, when fossilized, are fossils.

**Herbivore**: a plant-eating animal.

**Jurassic Period**: the interval of geological time between 206 and 144 million years ago.

**Mesozoic Era** (**Mesozoic, Secondary Era**): the interval of geological time between 248 and 65 million years ago.

**Pack**: a group of predator animals acting together to capture their prey.

**Paleontologist**: a scientist who studies and reconstructs the prehistoric life.

**Paleozoic Era** (**Paleozoic, Primary Era**): the interval of geological time between 570 and 248 million years ago.

**Predator**: an animal that preys on other animals for food.

**Raptor** (**raptorial**): a bird of prey, such as an eagle, hawk, falcon, or owl.

**Rectrix** (**plural rectrices**): any of the larger feathers in a bird's tail that are important in helping its flight direction.

**Scavenger**: an animal that eats dead animals.

**Skeleton**: a structure of an animal's body made of several different bones. One primary function is to protect delicate organs such as the brain, lungs, and heart.

**Skin**: the external, thin layer of the animal body. Skin cannot fossilize, unless it is covered by scales, feathers, or fur.

**Skull**: bones that protect the brain and the face.

**Teeth**: tough structures in the jaws used to hold, cut, and sometimes process food.

**Terrestrial**: living on land.

**Triassic Period**: the interval of geological time between 248 and 206 million years ago.

**Unearth**: to find something that was buried beneath the earth.

**Vertebrae**: the single bones of the backbone; they protect the spinal cord.

# DINOSAUR WEBSITES

**Dino Database**

www.dinodatabase.com

Get the latest news on dinosaur research and discoveries.
This site is pretty advanced, so you may need help from a teacher
or parent to find what you're looking for.

**Dinosaurs for Kids**

www.kidsdinos.com

There's basic information about most dinosaur types, and you can
play dinosaur games, vote for your favorite dinosaur, and learn
about the study of dinosaurs, paleontology.

**Dinosaur Train**

pbskids.org/dinosaurtrain

From the PBS show *Dinosaur Train*, you can watch videos,
print out pages to color, play games, and learn lots of facts about
so many dinosaurs!

**Discovery Channel Dinosaur Videos**

discovery.com/video-topics/other/other-topics-dinosaur-videos.htm
Watch almost 100 videos about the life of dinosaurs!

**The Natural History Museum**

www.nhm.ac.uk/kids-only/dinosaurs

Take a quiz to see how much you know about dinosaurs—or a quiz
to tell you what type of dinosaur you'd be! There's also
a fun directory of dinosaurs, including some cool 3-D views of
your favorites.

# MUSEUMS

**American Museum of Natural History**, New York, NY
www.amnh.org

**Carnegie Museum of Natural History**, Pittsburgh, PA
www.carnegiemnh.org

**Denver Museum of Nature and Science**, Denver, CO
www.dmns.org

**Dinosaur National Monument**, Dinosaur, CO
www.nps.gov/dino

**The Field Museum**, Chicago, IL
fieldmuseum.org

**University of California Museum of Paleontology**, Berkeley, CA
www.ucmp.berkeley.edu

**Museum of the Rockies**, Bozeman, MT
www.museumoftherockies.org

**National Museum of Natural History, Smithsonian Institution**,
Washington, DC
www.mnh.si.edu

**Royal Tyrrell Museum of Palaeontology**, Drumheller, Canada
www.tyrrellmuseum.com

**Sam Noble Museum of Natural History**, Norman, OK
www.snomnh.ou.edu

**Yale Peabody Museum of Natural History**, New Haven, CT
peabody.yale.edu

# INDEX

Page numbers in **boldface** are illustrations.